The Adventures of Jolie and Her Best Friends Hamilton and Bacorama

A Lesson for Freddie

Rhoda Starzyk and Jolie Robinson

PAGE PUBLISHING, INC.
Conneaut Lake, PA

First originally published by Page Publishing 2020

ISBN 978-1-64628-900-4 (pbk)
ISBN 978-1-64628-899-1 (digital)

Printed in the United States of America

To our families, who always support us in all we do.

"Yay! Nana's here!"

Jolie was so excited to see Nana pull up. Nana drove a minibus that had all the colors of the rainbow splashed on it and a big peace sign on the side. Jolie had once overheard her parents say that Nana drove the minibus because she was a "hippy." Jolie didn't know what that meant. She only knew that whenever Nana showed up, there was going to be an adventure. The bus was covered in all kinds of bumper stickers showing all the places where Nana had been—a lot of the places she had taken Jolie and Jolie's best friends, Hamilton and Bacorama.

Hamilton and Bacorama were pigs that Nana and Jolie had gotten from a rescue farm. When Jolie first saw them, they were small and skinny and kind of grayish from being sick. They had not been taken very good care of by their owner, but then they came to live with Jolie. With Nana's help, Jolie learned how to care for them and love them, and now they were healthy and pink and

Jolie's best friends. They did everything together, and Jolie would never consider going on any adventure without them. The best part of her friendship with Hamilton and Bacorama was that she could tell them anything. They never made fun of her if she was being scared or mad or acting silly, and they could talk! Nana said it was because Jolie was such a special girl, and the pigs knew they could trust Jolie. Jolie knew that Nana talked to animals all the time, and she must have passed that gift on to Jolie.

Today, Nana was picking them up and they were going camping! Jolie had been camping with Nana before, but this would be the first time for Hamilton and Bacorama. Jolie told them all about walking through the forest, looking for the different kinds of animals and plants, making s'mores by the fire at night and telling ghost stories, catching fireflies and swimming in the old swimming hole that Nana used to swim in when she was a little girl.

"This is going to be awesome!" exclaimed Bacorama. "Well, maybe all of it except the ghost stories."

"Oh, it'll be fun, no matter what," said Hamilton. "Nana always makes it fun."

They all piled into the minibus and off they headed. Along the way, they played games like I spy and made up jokes. Before they knew it, time had flown by, and they were pulling into their campsite. Nana hadn't told them what campsite they were going to, and when they pulled in, Jolie got so excited.

"Oh, Nana, you're the best!" she exclaimed.

Jolie had just told Nana last week how much she missed her squirrel friends, Squeak and Freddie. And now, Jolie saw that Nana had picked a campsite close to their home in the forest. Now she could introduce them to Hamilton and Bacorama. They were going to have such fun together!

The campsite was set in among tall pine trees. The trees towered over the campsites and provided shade for the campers and tents that were set up. While Nana set up their tents, Jolie, Hamilton, and Bacorama gathered firewood and went to the swimming hole to get some water. When everything was ready, they set off to their adventure.

7

Jolie showed them where she had made a fairy garden next to a tree that had fallen down. Some of the little ferns and plants she had put around were still there and so was the little stone path she had made. They cleaned it up and found some fresh green moss to put down so the fairies had a nice, soft place to sleep. Then they found some pretty flowers to put around to welcome the fairies back.

"Everyone knows how much fairies love flowers," said Jolie.

Next, Jolie led them on a trail through the woods and at the end, they came to a huge tree with a really big hole in it. Above the hole was a sign that read, Mrs. Hoot's Learning Academy.

"Wow," said Bacorama, bending over backward to look up to the top and falling over. "That's a really, really big tree. I bet it reaches to the moon! What is this place?"

"This must be the forest school," said Jolie. "My friends Squeak and Freddie have told me all about it, but I have never been here before. Mrs. Hoot is their teacher. They said she is really nice."

Suddenly, they heard a bell, and out from the hole in the big tree came all kinds of young animals: skunks, chipmunks, deer, birds, rabbits, toads, and Jolie's friends, Squeak and Freddie.

"Jolie, Jolie, what are you doing here?" They rushed over to her and gave her a big hug.

MRS. HOOT'S
LEARNING ACADEMY

Ringggggg

RRRRRinng99

"Nana brought us camping," said Jolie. "We're going to be here for a few days."

"Yay!" yelled Squeak.

"That's awesome," said Freddie. "We'll ask Mrs. Hoot if you can come to school tomorrow. We'll show you our classroom, and maybe you can eat with us tomorrow night, and we can show you our new clubhouse that Dad built us."

Jolie said, "That would be neat, but I brought my two friends with me. This is Hamilton and Bacorama. Do you think they could come too?"

"Sure," said Freddie. "I'll go ask Mrs. Hoot now." And off he scampered.

Squeak ran over to Hamilton and Bacorama, all excited about meeting new friends. She gave them a really big hug and said, "Oh, I just love meeting new friends. We are going to have so, so, so, so, so much fun. Come on, and I'll show you where we play hide-and-seek."

Off she ran, running under bushes and over fallen trees and rocks. They had a hard time keeping up and were out of breath when they caught up to her.

"Boy," huffed Hamilton. "You sure can run fast."

"Fastest in my class," she said, just a little proud of herself.

"You must be really great at racing," puffed Bacorama.

Just then, Freddie bounded over to where they were catching their breath as they watched Squeak jump from tree to tree.

"She makes me tired just watching her," said Jolie as she sat down to rest.

"Oh, that's just Squeak, always running here and there," said Freddie. "I just spoke to Mrs. Hoot, and she is very excited about you visiting with us tomorrow at school. Do you think your Nana will let you?"

Jolie replied, "I'm sure she will. After all, she brought us here to visit with you, and Nana loves us to learn new things too. What a better way than to go to school with you?"

13

"I never thought I'd be excited to be going to school," said Hamilton.

"We're going to go back to camp now," said Jolie. "I told Nana we wouldn't be long, and I don't want her to worry. Why don't you come with us, and we can all ask Nana together?"

As they all hurried back to camp, Squeak ran ahead of them, then ran back, then ran ahead again.

"I don't know how she does it," said Bacorama, knowing that his short, little legs would never be able to keep up with her.

The last time she came back, Nana was with her. Freddie ran ahead to say hi.

"It's so good to see you again, Squeak and Freddie. My, how you've grown. Your tails get fluffier and fluffier every time I see you." Then to Jolie, Nana said, "I hear you are going to visit your friends at school tomorrow."

"How did you know I was going to ask you?" replied Jolie.

"I ran into Mrs. Hoot while I was taking a walk looking for new and interesting plants, and she asked if it would be okay," said Nana.

"You know Mrs. Hoot?" asked Hamilton.

"Nana knows everybody," said Jolie. "She has been coming camping here since she was a little girl and has made friends with all the forest animals."

"Wow, you must be really old," said Bacorama.

"I may be old, but I bet I can beat you back to camp," replied Nana, and off she ran.

They were so surprised at seeing her run that they just stood there startled, and she had a big head start before they ran after her. That night after dinner, they settled down in front of the campfire, and Nana told them about the things she used to do there when she was a little girl.

"I used to go berry picking in the wild blueberry and raspberry patches. I used to play with my animal friends and make fairy gardens just like Jolie does. I also used to go swimming down at the old swimming hole. There used to be a tire swing there that you could climb on, and it would swing way out over the water, then I would jump off and swim ashore. It was so much fun. There was also a canoe that I used to paddle around, pretending I was on great adventures."

"Oh Nana, I remember the tire swing but not the canoe. Do you think we could try the swing while we are here?" asked Jolie.

"I'll have to make sure it's safe first. While you are visiting the school tomorrow, I will go check it out," replied Nana. "As for the canoe, that hasn't been there for a very long time, but I did bring an inflatable raft you can use."

"Yay," said Hamilton. "This is the best vacation ever! Can we tell ghost stories now?" asked Hamilton.

Nana noticed that Bacorama looked uncomfortable with that idea, and Jolie was trying to hide a yawn.

"We had a long ride today and a lot of excitement setting up camp and seeing our friends again. How about we save that for tomorrow night?"

"That's a great idea," said Bacorama, looking very relieved. "I am tired."

"So am I," said Jolie, stifling another yawn. "Let's get a good night sleep, so we can be wide awake for Mrs. Hoot's class tomorrow."

So, they climbed into their tent and were fast asleep in no time.

The next morning, Jolie, Hamilton, and Bacorama set out to pick some blueberries for their pancakes that Nana was making for their breakfast. They found a few bushes with the biggest, juiciest blueberries they had ever seen.

"Bacorama, I think you've put more in your mouth than in the bucket," said Jolie, popping some in her mouth too.

"I can't help it," said Bacorama with blueberry juice running down his chin. "They are so sweet and so yummy."

After breakfast, they set out for the forest school. Freddie met them on the path.

"Where is Squeak?" asked Jolie.

"Oh, when we got home last night, a new family had moved into the tree next door. They have a little squirrel named Pip, and Squeak was going to walk to school with her today," replied Freddie.

"That was nice of her," said Hamilton.

"I suppose," said Freddie.

Jolie could tell that Freddie wasn't very happy about Squeak not being there, but she decided not to say anything about it.

18

When they got to the school, all the animals were making their way in and finding their seats. Jolie, Hamilton, and Bacorama had never been inside a tree before. When they walked into the big hole that was the front door, they looked way up. You could see almost to the top of the tree. Bacorama bent over backward so far to see the top that he fell over again.

"Gosh," he said.

Mrs. Hoot greeted them when they came inside. "It's so nice to meet you at last," she said. "Squeak and Freddie talk about you all the time, and, of course, so does your Nana every time I see her."

Mrs. Hoot was a beautiful Barn Owl, all brown and gold. Her eyes looked very wise, and Jolie was sure that she saw everything that went on in her classroom, as she demonstrated when she told the skunk twins to stop raising their tails at each other. The twins were behind her. Seeing Jolie's surprised look, she said, "Sometimes you just know whoooo is doing what."

Right about then, Squeak bounded over, all excited to see them. With her, but lagging behind somewhat and seeming very shy, was a cute, little black squirrel.

"This is my new friend Pip," she gushed. "Pip is awesome. She can do everything. She can climb really high, and she can run really fast. Not as fast as me, but still really fast. And she is awesome at hide-and-seek."

Squeak had to stop talking because she was out of breath. Jolie could see that Freddie was standing off by himself, and he looked upset. By now, it was time to find their seats and get settled in.

Mrs. Hoot's classroom was really neat. Jolie, Hamilton, and Bacorama had never seen anything like it before. Mrs. Hoot sat up on a branch in front of the room to teach. The animal children sat on chairs that were made out of small logs, and their desk was one long log in front of them. Their pencils were shaped like little twigs, and their paper was the bark from the trees.

"We have guests today," said Mrs. Hoot. "I thought it would be nice to tell them what we learn in class. Whoooo wants to go first?"

The animals were so excited to have visitors. They wanted to share everything they do, and they raised their little paws and wings high.

"Okay, Jessie and Jacob, you go first. Tell us one thing we are taught in school," said Mrs. Hoot. Jessie and Jacob were the skunk twins that she had spoken to before.

"Well," said Jessie. "We learn to…"

"Not walk in the road when there are cars coming," finished Jacob.

"Oh, I was going to say that," said Jessie as she raised her tail at him.

"Now, now, you two," said Mrs. Hoot. "Let's not have any fighting please. Remember what happened the last time."

"Yeah, the school smelled for a week," giggled Squeak to Pip. Everyone started laughing. Freddie just sat there, looking bothered.

"Whoooo else wants to share with our visitors?" Mrs. Hoot asked. "Okay, Chester," Mrs. Hoot said to a little chipmunk.

"Those of us who can, are taught to climb," squeaked Chester.

"And others of us who can't climb," said Rebecca Robin, "learn how to fly."

"That's right Rebecca," said Mrs. Hoot. "But remember to raise your wing before answering. Whoooo's next?" asked Mrs. Hoot.

The animals took turns telling Jolie, Hamilton, and Bacorama how they learned to gather food for the winter, stay away from predators and find shelter in a storm.

Then Jolie raised her hand.

"Yes, Jolie, do you have a question?" asked Mrs. Hoot.

"Well, not really a question. I didn't realize that you had to learn all those things. I guess I just thought you knew how to do them."

"Well," said Mrs. Hoot. "Do you know how to walk and talk when you are born? Do you know how to play and eat? Don't you have people helping you learn those things?"

"Yeah," said Jolie. "I guess we do."

"Well, it's the same with animals. We have to learn too."

"Your school is really neat, Mrs. Hoot. Thank you for letting us visit with you," said Jolie.

"You are more than welcome, my dear. You are welcome back anytime," said Mrs. Hoot.

That afternoon, after school, Jolie, Hamilton, Bacorama, Squeak, Freddie, and Pip went to the swimming hole. At first, Pip didn't want to go because she didn't really know anyone and was shy, but Squeak talked her into it.

"We'll have such great fun!" exclaimed Squeak. "You just have to come, doesn't she, Freddie?"

"She can come if she wants to or not. It's up to her," said Freddie sadly, shuffling along the path behind them.

In the end, she decided to go. The old tire swing wasn't there any longer, but they played in the inflatable raft that Nana had brought. There was a small island in the middle of the water that they paddled over to, and they pretended to be pirates looking for a treasure. They used branches for swords and said "argh" a lot. Freddie went with them but mostly played by himself, skipping stones and exploring different trees. At one point, Jolie asked Freddie if anything was wrong.

"Ah, nothing," said Freddie.

After exploring, they went swimming. All except Freddie who just sat on a tree stump, watching gloomily. Though Jolie, Hamilton, and Bacorama couldn't use the tire swing, there was a big rock that sat at the deep side of the water's edge, and they jumped off that. Squeak and Pip climbed a tree and jumped off a branch that hung out over the water. They tried to see who could make the biggest splash. Hamilton won. They all had such great fun except Freddie.

When it was time for dinner, they all headed back to camp to find Mr. and Mrs. Squirrel and Mrs. Hoot there to join them. Pip headed home to have dinner with her family.

"How was your day?" asked Mrs. Squirrel.

"It was fantastic," said Squeak excitedly. "First, they came to school with us and then we went to play at the swimming hole. That was so much fun. We played pirates, and Pip was such a good pirate. She is good with a sword and finding things, and she can climb really high, almost as high as me, and she helped us row the raft over to the island." The more Squeak had to say, the quicker she talked. "She is a great swimmer too. And boy can she jump. She is so neat. We had such a great time. Didn't we Freddie?"

"Pip Pip Pip. That's all I hear. How great Pip is. How awesome Pip is. She can do this and she can do that," said Freddie angrily. "I'm tired of hearing her name. I can't even believe you play with her. She's different from us. She's a black squirrel. Why would you even want to be her friend?"

Everyone just stared at Freddie. They couldn't believe what he just said.

"Frederick Squirrel," Mr. Squirrel said in his strict father's voice.

Freddie knew he had gone too far when his dad used his full name. But he didn't care.

Mrs. Squirrel said to Freddie, "What difference does it make that she is a black squirrel? Your dad is a gray squirrel, and I am a red squirrel. And you and Squeak are different colors."

"That's different." Freddie pouted. "We're all related."

"Well, we are now, but before your father and I were married, we weren't related. What would have happened if I felt that same way then and didn't want to be around a gray squirrel? Then your dad wouldn't be your dad now, and Squeak wouldn't be your sister."

"Well, that would be okay with me. I mean Squeak not being my sister. Who needs her anyway!" shouted Freddie as he ran off.

Poor Squeak was so shocked at what had just happened that she just stood there and cried. "What did I do?" she sobbed.

"There, there my dear," said Mrs. Hoot as she comforted Squeak, wrapping her warm wings around her. "Everything will be okay."

"No, it won't," sniffled Squeak. "Freddie doesn't want to be my brother anymore. I don't know what I will do. He is my best friend." And with that, she cried even harder.

"Well, we have to go find him. It's getting dark," said Nana.

"Nana, I think I know where he is. Can I go talk to him?" asked Jolie. "I think I know what's wrong."

"Okay," said Nana. "But don't be too long. I don't want you wandering in the woods at night."

"I won't be by myself. Hamilton and Bacorama will be with me."

"We will?" squealed Bacorama, not liking the idea of walking through the woods in the dark.

"Yes," said Jolie. "I'm going to need your help."

Jolie borrowed Nana's flashlight, and they headed out.

"Where are we going?" asked Hamilton.

"To the one place I know Freddie will be," said Jolie.

"Where is that?" squeaked Bacorama, looking around nervously, not liking the shadows that the flashlight was making on the trees.

"Well, where do I go when I'm upset or hurt?" asked Jolie.

Hamilton and Bacorama thought for a minute and said together, "Your secret hiding place."

"Right," said Jolie. "And I think I know where Freddie's secret hiding place is."

Jolie led them through the woods, very careful to stay on the path so that they didn't get lost. It wasn't long before they came to a beautiful oak tree. Partway up the tree, Jolie shone the light, and they could see a squirrel nest.

"This is Freddie and Squeak's home," she said.

Then Jolie moved the light over the branches on the tree until she found what she was looking for. Partly hidden under the leaves, farther up the tree, and out on a sturdy branch was what looked like another nest.

"That must be their new clubhouse," said Jolie. "Freddie was telling me all about it."

There was movement up on the branch, and suddenly, a sign appeared on the branch just below the clubhouse that said: Only red and gray squirrels allowed.

"Yup," said Hamilton. "I think you're right about that."

Jolie said, "You guys stay right here. I'm going up to talk to Freddie."

"You're what?" squealed Bacorama.

"Don't worry. I learned to climb trees from Nana. This will be a piece of cake."

Even Hamilton seemed unsure about this plan, but as Jolie started climbing, it was obvious that she knew what she was doing. Her hands and feet seemed to know exactly where to go, and she climbed right up.

"That Jolie is full of surprises," said Hamilton.

Jolie reached the branch that the clubhouse was on and scooted over to sit next to the nest. The full moon helped to light up the branch, and Jolie could see something moving in the clubhouse.

"Freddie?" called Jolie "Are you in there?"

"No," said a small, sad voice.

"Freddie, I know you're there. I just want to talk."

"I don't want to talk," said Freddie. "I just want to be by myself."

"Okay," said Jolie "I'll leave you alone, but I just want to say one thing. I know what is bothering you, and I know that it has nothing to do with Pip being a black squirrel."

"Oh, yes it does," said Freddie. "I don't think Squeak should play with her. She's different, and she doesn't belong."

"You don't mean that," said Jolie.

"Yes, I do," said Freddie angrily.

"I know you don't, and I'll tell you how I know that you don't mean that," said Jolie. "You don't care that people and animals are different. You became my friend almost as soon as we met, and I'm different. My daddy is black, and my mommy is white. Nana is white, and I have brown skin. That never bothered you. You became friends right away with Hamilton and Bacorama, and they are pigs. And I know for a fact that Chester is one of your best friends, and he is a chipmunk," explained Jolie.

"That's different," said Freddie.

"How?" asked Jolie.

"It just is," frowned Freddie.

"I have been watching you all day since Squeak started hanging out with Pip and showing her around, and I have noticed that the more Squeak and Pip did together, the sadder you got and the grumpier you got," said Jolie.

"I'm not grumpy," pouted Freddie.

"No, not much," said Jolie rolling her eyes. "I think you are jealous of their new friendship."

"I am not," said Freddie with tears in his eyes.

"Well, if you are, you don't need to be. It was very nice of Squeak to help Pip. To show her around and introduce her to other animals so that she can make new friends," said Jolie.

"But does she have to talk about her all the time? Pip this and Pip that, and she runs so fast and climbs so high and blah, blah, blah. She's not that great," whined Freddie.

"It won't last," said Jolie. "Squeak is just excited about someone new in the neighborhood. If I'm not mistaken, you were the same when Chester moved in."

"I wasn't like that!" said Freddie.

"Maybe not that excited, but that's just the way Squeak is. She gets excited about everything."

"That's for sure," mumbled Freddie.

"But you used to talk about Chester all the time. How he could find the best acorns and how he could stuff so many in his mouth he looked like a balloon."

"He really can," giggled Freddie. "He looks so funny when he does that, and he makes me laugh. I have never seen anything like it."

"Right," said Jolie. "And that's the same way with Squeak. There are some things that Pip is good at, and right now, it's new and exciting to Squeak, and she likes to tell everyone about them," explained Jolie. "I know it seems like she's spending a lot of time with Pip and maybe not as much with you, but I also know that if you asked to go along, they would love to have you play with them. And I also know that you spent a lot of time with Chester, too, but Squeak didn't get jealous. She found other things to do and other animals to play with because she knew it was important that you help Chester fit in. She is very proud of her big brother."

Freddie was quiet for a long time.

"Oh man, Jolie," whispered Freddie. "I wasn't very nice and I made a mess of things, and now I don't know how to fix it."

"Oh, fixing it is easy," said Jolie. "It all starts with saying you're sorry. Nana always says that you can fix anything if you really want to and if you really mean it."

"I really do want to," said Freddie.

"Okay," said Jolie. "Then step one is to get out of this tree and go talk to Squeak and your parents."

"Oh no!" cried Freddie. "My parents! I said some bad things to them too. I'm in so much trouble."

"I bet things aren't as bad as you think they are," said Jolie. "Let's go make this right."

They had just climbed down from the tree when Freddie turned around quickly and started going back up. Bacorama started jumping around nervously.

"What's the matter? What did he see? Why is he running away?"

"I'm not running away," said Freddie. "I need to do something first."

With Jolie holding the flashlight so that they could see where Freddie was going, he climbed back to the clubhouse, took the sign down and ripped it up.

"Sure don't need this anymore or ever again," said Freddie. Freddie went into the clubhouse, and after a minute or two, brought out a new sign that he put on the clubhouse. It read: Clubhouse for Everyone.

"Nice," said Hamilton.

"Awesome!" yelled Bacorama, hoof pumping the air.

They had been away for quite a while, and Jolie knew that Nana would be coming looking for them, so they hurried back to camp. Mr. and Mrs. Squirrel, Mrs. Hoot, and Nana were sitting around the campfire, talking. Squeak was sitting away from the fire by herself giving a sniff and wiping away tears every once in a while.

When they walked into the light of the fire, Freddie went right up to his parents and said, "Mom, Dad, I have something to say to you, but would you give me a minute to talk to Squeak for a minute?"

They looked at each other then nodded. Freddie walked over to where Squeak was sitting. He walked up to her and gave her a friendly nudge.

"Hi," he said.

"Go away," cried Squeak. "I don't want to talk to you."

Freddie looked over at Jolie, and she gave him a thumbs-up.

"You can do this," she whispered.

"Squeak, I'm sorry. I didn't mean anything that I said. Jolie helped me to see that I was acting like that because I was jealous of your new friendship with Pip. I was afraid you would want to stop doing things with me and just want to hang out with her. And so, I said things that I shouldn't have. I don't care that Pip is a black squirrel. That doesn't matter to me at all. And I'm glad that you are my sister. I wouldn't want a different one. You always make me laugh, and you're fun to play with, and you're nice to everyone. You make me very proud to be your brother."

Squeak was facing away from Freddie when he was talking, and when he was done, she just sat there, not saying anything. She sat quiet for a long time, and Freddie started getting nervous. Maybe she didn't hear him. Maybe she wasn't going to forgive him. Then what would he do?

"Squeak," said Freddie quietly. "Please forgive me. Please don't be mad at me anymore."

Then suddenly Squeak whirled around and threw her arms around Freddie. "Oh Freddie," she squealed. "Of course, I forgive you. Of course, I'm not mad at you. How can I be mad at you? You're my big brother. I love you and I always will." Squeak started chattering quickly. "I can't wait until tomorrow. I can't wait to tell Pip all about my big brother and all the awesome things he can do. I'll tell her how brave you are and how strong you are. How you can carry more acorns than anyone I know, well, except for Chester. Man, he can fit a lot into his mouth. He makes me laugh."

"Okay, okay," said Freddie. "I'm glad you forgive me, but you're making my ears hurt."

"You aren't the only one," said Bacorama, putting his hoofs over his ears.

Everyone laughed. Freddie went over to his parents.

"Mom and Dad, I'm sorry for what I said and for how I acted. What someone's color is or how different they are doesn't matter, and I'm lucky to have parents like you. I am sorry."

"Thank you for apologizing," said Mr. Squirrel. "It certainly helps to fix things, especially since you seem to mean it."

"I really do. What I said was wrong," said Freddie.

"Well," said Nana. "I'm glad that was able to be straightened out. Like I say, there isn't anything that can't be fixed with an apology. Now, how about some s'mores and ghost stories."

"Ghost stories!" Bacorama quivered. "Okay, but only if I can sit next to Nana, so that she doesn't get scared.

"Thank you, Bacorama." Nana smiled. "That's a great idea."

The End

About the Authors

Rhoda grew up in the Adirondack Mountains and moved to the Poughkeepsie area in 1978 where she held various jobs and presently works as a legal secretary. Rhoda lives among the hay and cornfields near the Hudson River in mid-state New York with her husband Ted and their two mischievous black cats, Puc and Pandora. They have three children and a wonderful granddaughter named Jolie who has inspired Rhoda's stories through her vivid imagination. She loves to write, spend time with her family, garden, rummage through flea markets, and undertake any project that allows her to use her creativity.

Jolie is an amazing seven-year-old who has been writing stories with her Nana since she first imagined Hamilton and Bacorama when she was three years old. Jolie loves school, reading, and being with her mom and dad and their two shy cats, Naveen and Tiana.

CPSIA information can be obtained
at www.ICGtesting.com
Printed in the USA
LVHW051409150520
655582LV00008B/354